THE
MAN
Raymond Briggs

Red Fox

After three days, fish and visitors begin to stink.

CHINESE PROVERB

A Red Fox Book

Published by Random House Children's Books
20 Vauxhall Bridge Road, London SW1V 2SA

A division of Random House UK Ltd
London Melbourne Sydney Auckland
Johannesburg and agencies throughout the world

Copyright © 1992 Raymond Briggs

1 3 5 7 9 10 8 6 4 2

First published in Great Britain by Julia MacRae

Red Fox edition 1994

Printed in China

RANDOM HOUSE UK Limited Reg. No. 954009

ISBN 0 09 910881 X

MONDAY

Here! Here, boy.
I'm dying for a pee -

You'd better not go to the bathroom.
My parents -
Can't you do it out of the window?

No! It's not dignified.
Haven't you got a potty or something?

You could do it in my paint water jar.

OK. Pass it over.
Right.
Now get me something to stand on.

Aah! Bliss!

I am too old to believe
in this kind of thing.

What happened to your clothes?

It's a long story. Bit embarrassing …
What about that grub?

I'll see what I can do.

Here! Take the jam jar with you.
Put it down the lav. And wash it out properly.
Hygiene at all times, remember.
And wash your hands before you get my grub.
That's another thing - I wouldn't mind a bath.
But get the grub first.

Look … I'm not dreaming, am I?
This <u>has</u> changed colour.
You <u>are</u> real.

Just stop jabbering tripe and get that grub.

Here's the grub.

What you got?

Bran flakes -

I prefer Coco-Pops.

Bread and -

Ugh! <u>Brown</u> bread!
Horrible wholemeal!
All lumpy and stodgy with mucky bits in.
I like sliced white - Mother's Pride!

Mum won't have it in the house.

You'll have to get some.
I can't eat horrible wholemeal.
Gives me the trots.

JOHN!

Yes, Mum?

WHAT HAVE YOU BEEN UP TO IN THE KITCHEN?

Er … just a bit of bread, Mum.

YOU NEEDN'T THINK YOU'RE GOING TO START EATING BREAKFAST UPSTAIRS.

Oh, no, Mum. I was hungry …
just tidying my room …
before breakfast … like you said …

**Ugh! <u>Jelly</u> marmalade. No good.
Listen! Always get Frank Cooper's
Oxford Marmalade.
Write it down.**

That's a brilliant way to eat
branflakes.
Never seen anyone eat them
one at a time before.

**You get more sugar that way, see?
Like Frosties.
Any tea?**

Er … yes. OK.

**Nice and strong.
Got PG Tips?**

Mum always has Darjeeling
and Earl Grey.

**Bah! Rubbish!
Old maids' tea.
Mimsy wee-wee.
Always get PG Tips.**

I've made it in a mug.
I don't see how you're going to drink it.

**Rotten milk in this.
Skimmed muck, isn't it?**

Yes, Mum says -

**Get Gold Top. Channel Islands Jersey Milk.
That's real milk.
I can't drink out of this thing.**

I know!
There's a little glass with a handle.
Wait.

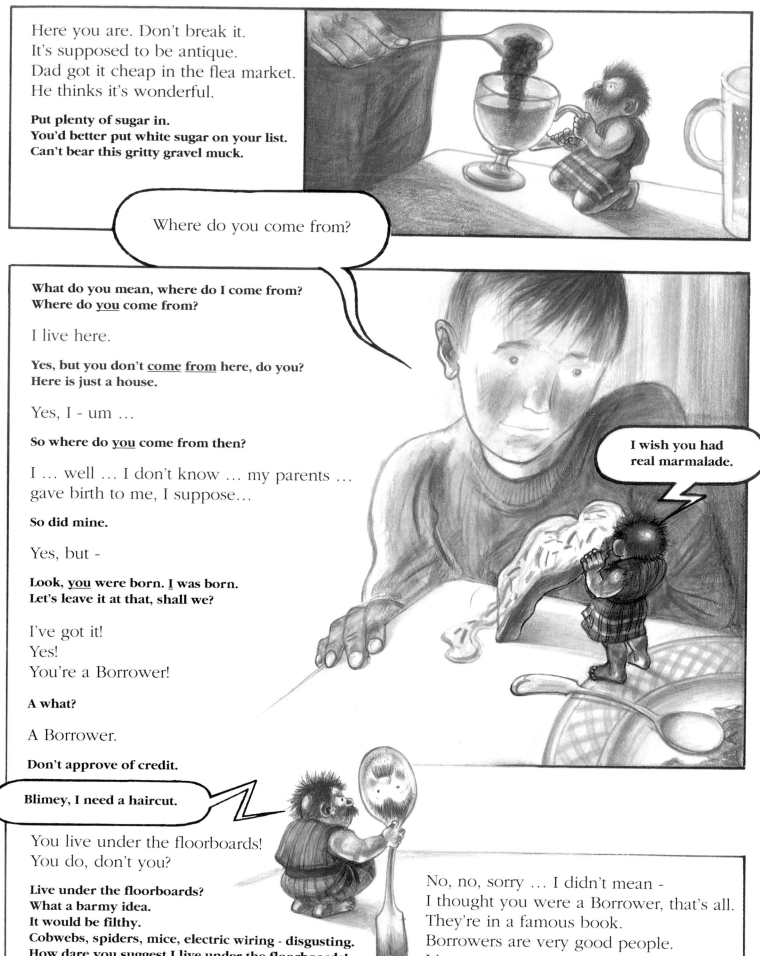

Here you are. Don't break it.
It's supposed to be antique.
Dad got it cheap in the flea market.
He thinks it's wonderful.

Put plenty of sugar in.
You'd better put white sugar on your list.
Can't bear this gritty gravel muck.

Where do you come from?

What do you mean, where do I come from?
Where do _you_ come from?

I live here.

Yes, but you don't _come from_ here, do you?
Here is just a house.

Yes, I - um …

So where do _you_ come from then?

I … well … I don't know … my parents …
gave birth to me, I suppose…

So did mine.

Yes, but -

Look, _you_ were born. _I_ was born.
Let's leave it at that, shall we?

I've got it!
Yes!
You're a Borrower!

A what?

A Borrower.

Don't approve of credit.

I wish you had
real marmalade.

Blimey, I need a haircut.

You live under the floorboards!
You do, don't you?

Live under the floorboards?
What a barmy idea.
It would be filthy.
Cobwebs, spiders, mice, electric wiring - disgusting.
How dare you suggest I live under the floorboards!
You are prejudiced, aren't you?
Just because I am smaller than you, you think I must
live in small, dirty places - like a rat!

No, no, sorry … I didn't mean -
I thought you were a Borrower, that's all.
They're in a famous book.
Borrowers are very good people.
It's a great story.

Pah! Stories!
I hate them.

Here! See that old fur glove with holes in?
It's worn out.
Give us the scissors.

Now! That's it!
Fur boots and fur underpants.
Lovely!
Give us that pin.

Any more of my clothes you'd like to cut up?

Not for the moment.

I suppose you must be from Space?
Like ET?

**Eetee?
Never heard of it.**

It's a film.
A famous film.

**Don't like films.
Too big.**

But you <u>are</u> from Space.
You must be.

Can you really imagine <u>me</u> in Space?

Er … no.
Come to think of it. No.

Where am I going to sleep?

Sleep?

Yes.

What!
You're staying?

**Well, it's raining.
Your parents had better not see me.
You never know how adults will react to people like me.
Some of them make straight for the Hoover and the Dettol.
Children are more reliable, unless they are crawlers,
then they try and eat me or pull my legs off.
So where am I going to sleep?**

Um … well …

**This glove is OK for a sleeping bag,
but I need a bit of privacy.**

You could use my Secrets
Cupboard. It's Top Secret.
Even Mum doesn't look in here.
She's promised.

Is it clean?

It's the safest place.
I'll clean it out for you.

What a glory hole.

Hey! What about this?
Table tennis net!
I could pin it up either side in the cupboard.
Make you a hammock.
OK?

Yeah! That's good.
You're a brilliant boy.

I've got you a bit of carpet.

Is it red?

No. Grey-green.

I prefer red.

I'M OFF NOW, JOHN.
WON'T BE LONG.

OK. 'Bye, Mum.

Coast clear now.
How about this bath?

Oh … er … yes, OK.
Come and see.

No!
Not in your bath!
Far too dangerous. Lift me out.
You'll have to get me something -
a container.

Well … um … what, exactly?

Use your imagination, boy!
Look in the kitchen.

OK.

What about this?
It's heat proof.

Hmm … not very dignified.
Too transparent.
Never mind. It'll do.
Get some hot water.
And some cold.
So's to make a nice mix.

More hot.
Whoa! Not too much.
More cold.
Steady!
That's OK.
Got any Bath Foam?
I like Avocado or Peach Blossom.

We've only got Woodland Pine.

Never mind.
It'll have to do till you go shopping.
Mix it in. Lovely!
Put a pile of books to make steps.
That's what I usually do.

Usually do?
Do you do this often?

Of course. All the time.
I haven't got a place of my own.
We have to move about …
Have to keep on the move.
We can't live on our own, see?
Getting old now, I'd like to settle down …
but it never works out …

Oh?

three days …

What?

that's about the limit.

What is?

Never mind, boy.
I'm just rambling.

What am I going to do if Mum comes in?

Bung the bowl in the Secrets Cupboard with me in it.
Any shampoo?

There's Mum's "Caresse" or Dad's
Medicated Anti-Dandruff.

Give me the "Caresse".
I've got very sensitive skin.
You can do my hair.
Not too rough mind.
Be nice and gentle.

You've got a bald patch.

Haven't!
Considering my age, I'm hardly bald at all.

How old are you?

Very personal question.

Well?

We're on a different time scale to you.

What, like cats and dogs?

Yes. Sort of.

One year of ours equals
seven years in a dog?

That sort of thing.

So how old <u>are</u> you?

In our time or your time?

Your time. No! Ours.

I can't work it out.

What?

I've forgotten the ratio.

Your voice is very deep, isn't it?
Sounds almost like a normal person.

I <u>am</u> a normal person!

I thought tiny people had squeaky voices.

I am <u>not</u> tiny!
My voice is <u>not</u> squeaky!

Don't shout.
Mum will be back soon.

Now you can give me a hair cut.

I'm not a hairdresser!

Keep still!

Just mind
my little ears.

Look … um … I suppose … are you …
um -

Split it out, boy!

Well, don't be offended, but … er …
could it be that you are … a fairy?

A WHAT!

Oh sorry … I didn't mean -

How dare you!
Do I look like a blasted fairy?

No, no, not a bit -

Do you see any gossamer wings?

No, no, of course not … sorry …
it's just that you are …
well … tiny.

All size is relative.

But fairies are tiny people.

I am not tiny!
I am the size I am.
You are the size you are.
Pass the hair gel.

Haven't you got tiny
fingernails! Let's look.
They are amazing.

Yes. They always say
I've got nice hands.

Just like a teensy-weensy
new-born baby! Ever so sweet!

Shut up!

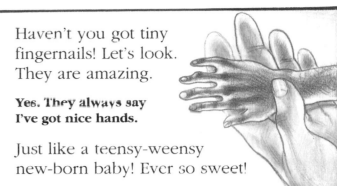

You can rig me up a shower later.
Use a pepper pot or a caster sugar sprinkler.
This towel is too big.

I know! Wait!

Ooh! Lovely!

You're very hairy, aren't you?

Don't make personal remarks.

Yuk!
You've got hair all down your back!
You're like an animal.

Careful!
Turn it down!

HA! HA! HA!

Switch it off!

I think I'll have a kip now.
Feel a bit knackered.
Do you mind keeping quiet for a bit?

No, no, not at all.
You go ahead.

Leave me the door open for some air.

Yes, of course.
I'll … er … go downstairs.
Got to go shopping anyway.

I'll have a cup of tea later.

Yes … yes … OK.

Got the list?

Yes.

Don't forget the Frank Cooper's Oxford.

No, OK.

Just a minute

Yes?

Before you go shopping -
Come here, boy. Pick me up.
Now listen. This is serious.

OK. I'm listening.

You've got to swear - not to tell <u>anyone</u> about me.

OK. I swear.

No one at all.
Not your mother. Not your father.
Not your friends.
No one.
TOP SECRET!

OK.

Remember - a secret is not a secret if more than two people know it.

Right.

No word to the Authorities -

Authorities?

Yes.
School, Town Council, DHSS, Police - that mob.
Nor the busybodies -

Busybodies?

Yes. Prodnoses, nosy parkers, tripe merchants - mucky newspapers, tatty magazines, soppy book publishers, twerp television, jabbering local radio - manufacturers and distributors of tripe by the ton. Tell <u>them</u> I'm here and they'll never let you alone. Or me. You'll be famous for a day and I'll be a comic turn. Our lives will be ruined.

So <u>swear</u>!

I swear.

Here -

Ouch!

Blood brothers!
United in blood and secrecy!

IS THAT YOU, JOHN?

She's back!
Yes, Mum.

WHO ARE YOU TALKING TO?

Oh … er … no one - no one at all.

I THOUGHT I HEARD VOICES?

Oh … er … um -

HAVE YOU STARTED TALKING TO YOURSELF?

No!

Well … yes, in a way.
I'm … er … writing a play …

OH YES?

Have to try out the lines … out loud.
Is there anything you'd like me to do, Mum?
Go down the shops?

NOW JUST WHAT ARE YOU FEELING GUILTY
ABOUT, JOHN?

Just going out, Mum.

JOHN!

Won't be long, Mum.

I got your grub.
Look - sliced white, PG Tips, white sugar
and Frank Cooper's Oxford Marmalade.

Brilliant!
You're a wonder-boy!

And I got a Gold Top off the milkman.

Channel Islands Milk?

Yes. Jersey. Full cream.

That's the stuff, boy!

Oh, by the way, I need a toothbrush.

That's OK.
We've always got spares in the bathroom.

Here -
Oh, sorry …

Never mind, boy.
Very kind of you.
I'm going to have another kip this afternoon.

You sleep a lot, don't you?

Well, it's winter, isn't it?

Evening, boy.

Evening, man.

Here, you couldn't get me
a bit of toilet paper, could you?

Yes, of course.

One bit will do.

What are you going to do
about the lavatory?
You can use ours but -

No.
Never go near those things.
Far too dangerous.
Fall in and you're a gonner.
Can't climb out, see?

What will you do, then?

Go up the wall, along the gutter,
then do it down the bog pipe.
Quite hygienic. Always do.

Come on, now.
Where <u>do</u> you come from, <u>please</u>?

"Whence came the Ice?
"Whose Womb hath gendered It?"

What?

Whose womb hath gendered <u>me</u>, eh?

TUESDAY

Hullo, little man.

Don't call me little!

But I don't know your name.

**Haven't got a name.
Never had one.**

Everyone's got a name.

**Oh?
Those gulls out there -
What are their names?**

Well, not gulls, no.
Not birds. Not animals.
But people have names.

**Well, we don't.
So there.**

Perhaps you are a sort of animal then.

**Perhaps I am.
You are a sort of animal, too.
What difference does it make?**

I don't know ... I ... um -
Can I get you something to eat?

What's for breakfast today?

Same as always - Bran Flakes,
Natural Yogurt and wholemeal bread.

**Pah! Health muck!
Don't you ever have egg and bacon?**

Dad has it on holiday sometimes.
If Mum lets him.

I'm dying for a sausage.

We never have sausages.

What about baked beans?

We have got those.
Unsweetened, of course.

In tomato sauce?

Yes, I think so ...

**Good.
I'll have that today. Beans on toast!
Look sharp. I'm starving.**

You'll have to wait till Mum goes out.

I can sprinkle them with sugar.

All that fuss and cooking and you've
only eaten six baked beans!
Six! And you say you're not tiny!

I'll fill up on toast and marmalade.

Hey, Man!
I've found a little brush on the music centre.
Just the job.

Good boy!

I'll have to put it back.
It's part of Dad's record deck stuff.

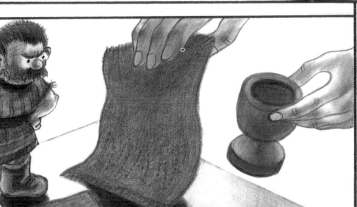

Look, Man!
I've made you a little towel.

I am <u>not</u> little!

All for your very own.
I've put your name on it, look.

Very nice.

And a teensy-weensy flannel.

Shut up!

And a wash basin

Listen, I've just had an idea …

Mmm?

Now don't be offended again -

Well?

Um … when you've got your clothes …

Yes?
Come on! Out with it!

Well, er … do you wear
a little red pointed hat?

OW!
That hurt!

What about school?
Did you go to school?

No.
Teach one another.
Not very efficient.
We're not well educated.
We get by.
You stick to your education, boy!
There's nothing worse
than being uneducated.

You miss so much in life.
It's like being only half alive.

I'll get you some more tea.

JOHN!

WHERE ON EARTH DID THIS EXPENSIVE MARMALADE COME FROM?

Oh, well … er … I got it, Mum.

YOU GOT IT! WHATEVER FOR?

Oh well … er … Darren says it's terrific. I thought I'd … try it.

WELL, I'M GLAD YOU CAN AFFORD IT.

Can I borrow your Walkman?

Yes, of course.
Here you are.

I like the Morning Service.

Radio Four … ninety-three point five …
Ah! Here we are.
Good stereo on FM, isn't it?

"ON-WARD CHRIST-IAN SOL-DIERS,
MAR-CHING AS TO WAR,
WITH THE CROSS OF JE-SUS
GO-ING ON BE-FORE."

Hey!
Hey, Man.
Must you sing?

What?

The whole point of a Walkman
is that you don't disturb other people.

It's the Morning Service.

I'm not religious.

Neither am I.
Not much anyway.
Pray a bit now and again.

Then why sing hymns?

Because it's the Morning Service.

"CHRIST THE ROY-AL MAR-TYR
LEADS A-GAINST THE FOE,
FOR-WARD IN-TO BA-TTLE
SEE HIS BAN-NERS GO."

Ssh!
I think Mum is still in!

ONWARD CHRISTIAN SOLDIERS

SSSH!

SONY WALKMAN FM/AM

MEGA BASS

Your Dad got any beer?
Guinness for preference.

No, sorry.
Dad only drinks wine.

Wine! Pah!
Sissie's drink.
Can you get me some?
I'm not a boozer.
Half a pint lasts me for weeks.

I'm too young to buy beer.

Can't you pinch it?

No!
I'm not a thief.

There must be very few of you.
I've never seen one of you before.

Too right.
Not many of us left.

You must be an Endangered Species, then.

We are not a Species!

Everyone is a Species.

We are people.

People are species.

Pah!
We're not.

So you don't exist, then?

You won't find us in the Record Books.

Then you must be an Undiscovered Species!

Undiscovered people, maybe.
Dying out, probably.

Yes!
That could be the answer!
My sister works for the Nature Conservancy.
She could get you conserved!

Don't want to be conserved.
Sounds like jam.

It's better than dying out, isn't it?

No, it isn't.
No one is putting me in a jam jar.

You wouldn't be in a jam jar, stupid.
They'd round you all up, give you a nice
warm place to live and look after you -

Sounds like an Old Folks' Home.
Or a Zoo.

No!
They'd help you.
Study you -

Don't want to be helped.
Don't want to be studied.
Want to be left to live.

Oh, all right.
Don't be helped, then.
Go on!
DIE OUT!
As if _I_ care.

Live your life?
Huh! That's a joke.
Your "life" consists of going round
people's houses … cadging … begging -
Yes! That's it!
You are a BEGGAR!

Am not.

Yes, you _are_!

Not dignified - a beggar.

Sorry … I didn't mean …

I'm too small to go to work.

Yes … sorry …

We have to get by … as best we can …

Yes, of course -
Look, come and sit on the sofa.
I'll put the telly on.

I want to _live_ my life!
No one is putting me in a MUSEUM!

Sorry …
don't cry …

I can't make
any money.

I try not to be too much trouble.

Yes, I know … I'll …
I'll get you something more to eat, shall I?
What would you like?

Marmalade.

Of course.
Any bread with it?

Toast.

OK.

And a choccy bicky.

OK.

Cup of tea would be nice.

Right.

**With lots of white sugar in.
And creamy milk.**

Don't push it, Man.

Nice and strong!

Look! It's for you.
I made it.

What is it?

A lavatory seat.
It will save you going up and down
the wall.

**Hmm … is it safe?
It's a long drop and there's no way out.**

Let's try it anyway.

**Lift me up, then.
See? I can't even get up there on my own.**

**No … sorry …
Don't feel safe …
It's a terrific drop.
If I fall, I've had it.**

Oh, OK.

**Get me down.
Nice of you, boy.
Very kind.
You're a good bloke.**

Got any chocolate?

No.
Mum's dead against sweets.

**Nip out and get us some After Eights, will you?
They're nice and thin for my little mouth.**

Um … I haven't got much money …
I don't suppose you -

"Naked came I into the world …"

I'll see what I can do.

**Don't get any nutty muck.
The nuts hurt my little teeth.**

Hey, Man! Man!
I've found some beer in the garage.
Left over from Christmas.
It's all dusty.

**Good boy!
My goodness, it's Guinness, too!**

And here's the After Eights.

**Oh goody!
Yum! Yum!**

**I really like this place.
Your Mum being out a lot.
Very clean.
Nice and warm.
Good central heating system.
Oh, by the way, I've turned
the thermostat up a bit.
Your bedroom's a bit chilly.
Hope that's OK.**

Oh yes … er … yes …
I should <u>think</u> so … um …
I don't suppose they'll notice.
I hope <u>Dad</u> doesn't …

I watched the football this afternoon.
While you were out shopping.

Oh?

Liverpool v Arsenal.

Oh.

Not interested?

No, not really.

What's your sport, then?

Don't like sport much.

What!
None of it?

Not really.

Blimey!
What do you like then?

Art.

ART!
Gor Blimey!
What sort of art?

Poetry and painting mostly.

POETRY and PAINTING! PAH!
Can't <u>stand</u> soppy ART!

Can't <u>stand</u> stupid SPORT!

SISSY!

DUMBO!

So … you're not a fairy, you're not an ET, you're not a gnome.
So what <u>are</u> you?

I'm me!
Just shut up!
It's insulting to be asked what I am all the time.
It implies I'm not human.

Well, you're not normal, are you?

Depends what you mean by normal.

You're not like <u>us</u>, are you?

Who is us?
<u>Your</u> little family?

Well, yes … if you like …

So are <u>you</u> the normal by which everyone is to be judged?

Well … um … I don't know really … no … I - I'll get you another biscuit, shall I?

Nearly five.
Mum will be back soon.
Better get you upstairs.

I wish <u>I</u> had a watch.

You can have my old digital if you like.

I'll get new batteries tomorrow.

JOHN!
DID I HEAR YOU SINGING HYMNS THIS MORNING?

Er … oh yes … yes … a bit -

I COULDN'T BELIEVE MY EARS.

No.
Ha ha … just a laugh, really -
it's in the play …

I'LL ENROL YOU FOR THE CHURCH CHOIR -

Oh no!
No, Mum, there's no need. Honestly -

Now look what you've done, you idiot!

She's pulling your leg … I think …

JOHN!
WHERE ON EARTH DID THIS
GOLD TOP MILK COME FROM?

Oh, it's me, Mum.
I thought I'd try it.
Darren says it's terrific.

IT SEEMS DARREN'S WORD IS LAW.

Aren't you lucky?

Why?

All these possessions!
Radio with cassette, electric clock,
Walkman, torch, calculator -

They're only gadgets.

I've got nothing!
Not even the clothes I stand up in.

I know. I'm sorry.

You've got a warm house, a bed with
a duvet, soft pillows, nice clothes -

Oh, don't go on.

What have I got?
An old sock to wear and an old mitten to sleep in!
My bed is a table tennis net held up with drawing pins!

Yes … well …
I'm sorry.
It's the best I can do.

I've never done any harm in the world, have I?

No. I shouldn't think so.

Then why should I be made to suffer?

I don't know, I -

Why is it other people get all the gravy?

Well

When is my turn coming?
Eh? Eh?
Answer me that!
When will I have a nice big car?
When will I own a whopping great house like this?
I'll never have enough to buy that rotten clock.

I gave you my watch.

Old one.
Doesn't work.

I'm getting new batteries.

Too big.
Don't want it.
Don't like second-hand goods.

I'm sorry things aren't …
more … equal.
I'd like to help, honestly.
I'm not sure what I can do …

I'll have a lie down now.
Bit of a kip.
Might pray a bit.

I'll get you some tea,
shall I?

Goody!
Yum! Yum!
Choccy bicky?

No!

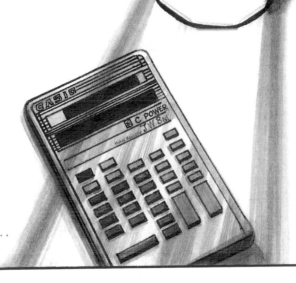

Can you get me a Bible?
It's all I ever read.
That and the Racing and Football Outlook.

Yes, I expect we've got one somewhere.
Mum quite likes Church …
now and again …
in small doses.

I admire the way you read in bed, boy.
I wish I could read in bed.
Can I borrow your torch?

"MAN THAT IS BORN OF WOMAN IS OF FEW DAYS
AND FULL OF TROUBLE. HE COMETH FORTH LIKE
A FLOWER AND IS CUT DOWN."
"HE FLEETH AS A SHADOW AND CONTINUETH NOT AND -"

Must you read aloud?

I can't read at all if I don't say it out loud.

Well, do you mind if I close the door, then?

I can't breathe!

Well, just read quietly, can't you?

OK.

"My flesh is clothed with worms and clods of dust;
my skin is broken, and become loathsome -"

Listen! I -

"Oh remember that my life is wind,
mine eye -"

SHUT UP!

I'm going down to watch the telly.

Lucky old you.
I'll just stay here and read the Bible …
with a torch …
in my table tennis net …
in a cupboard …
Don't worry about me.
You go ahead.
Enjoy yourself -

Just keep quiet!
Mum and Dad are both in, remember!

Have you been using the phone
in my parents' bedroom?

Er -

There was marmalade on the phone.

Oh ... er ... well -

Mum was furious.
I got the blame, of course.
It wasn't a long-distance call, was it?
Dad gets furious about phone bills.

Well ... it _was_ a sort of emergency.

Oh?
Who did you call?

**Very important.
My clothes ...**

Aha!
Go on!

Bit embarrassing ...

Yes?
Well?

It was engaged.

Was it?
Was it _really_?

Yes.

ZZZZZZZ...

Hey, Man!
Wake up, Man.

**Mmm ...
Wha ... what?**

You're snoring.

Never.

You were snoring fit to bust.

I never snore.

I'll have to close the door.

I'll suffocate!

Well, just don't snore then.

**Of course I won't.
I don't.**

Goodnight, Man.

ZZZZZZZZ...

Going out for some air.

Where will you go?

On the roofs.
Walk about.
Bit of fresh air.
It's OK at night. No birds.
Starlings are the worst.
They can rip your head off.

Be careful.
What about owls?

They don't bother with rooftops.
They work over the ground.
I like looking at the moon.
I might pray a bit.

I thought you weren't religious?

I'm not, but I feel … odd …
when I look at the moon.
Sometimes.
Don't worry, I won't pray for you.
It's _me_ I'm worried about.
Ta ta.

Go carefully.
Don't fall.
I'll wait up till you come back.
I'll make you a hot chocolate
in my Thermos.

WEDNESDAY

Any chance of a <u>fried</u> egg this morning, boy?

No.
I told you, I'm not allowed to fry.
I'll boil you one, if you like.

OK.
Better than nothing.
Make sure the yolk is runny.

Yes, yes, OK.

I don't like hard-boiled.

No, no, OK.

Make sure the white is firm, though.

Yes!

Can't bear a runny white.
Slimy. Horrible.

I do know how to boil an egg!

Into boiling water, then four minutes.

YES!

Got your watch?

YES!

Egg timer is best.
Can't beat the old egg timers.
Are they new-laid?

They are - "Honeysuckle-Farm-Fresh-
Free-Range-Organic-Fed …"

Health muck again.

What?

Nice!
Very nice.

Big end or little end?

Big end.

Crackle it or cut it?

Crackle it.

Good.
At least we agree
about <u>something</u>.

It's a yummy egg.
Wish it was fried.

Don't get it all over your beard!
It's all going down your front.
You're dribbling!

Never mind.

Never mind be blowed.
It's <u>my</u> sock you're dribbling on.
Oh, come here.
For someone who's always going
on about cleanliness, you're very
messy, aren't you?

We can't all live up to our ideals.
I do my little best.

You're very quiet, boy.

I'm a bit worried.

What about?

You.
What am I going to do with you?

<u>Do</u> with me!
How dare you!
<u>Do</u> with me, indeed!
Ever since I arrived you've done nothing but insult me.
NO ONE, but NO ONE, <u>DOES</u> <u>ANYTHING</u> WITH ME!
I DO IT!
Get it?
Suppose I said what am I going to <u>do</u> <u>with</u> you?
Who do you think you are? God?

But aren't you lost?

Lost?
Why should I be lost?

But you need someone to look after you.

No, I don't.

Yes, you do.
<u>I'm</u> looking after you now.

Yes, but you like doing it.

Maybe, but where would you be without me, eh?

Somewhere else, of course.

Exploiting someone else, I suppose?

Exploiting is not the word for what I do.

What would you call it then?

Do you <u>feel</u> exploited?

Well …
No, not really.

But you'd rather I left?

No.
Oh no. Don't go.

So you prefer me to stay?

Yes.

You like having me here?

Oh yes. Yes, of course.
It's terrific.

**There you are then.
More beer.**

Hold it steady, now.
And don't slop it.

See? You couldn't pour this.
You need me.
You need me more than I need you.

No, I don't -

I feed you!
Without me you'd starve.

**No, I wouldn't.
I'd find someone else.
There's plenty of you.
You're two a penny.
There's very few of me.
I am a rarity.
<u>You</u> are common.
<u>I</u> am almost unique.**

Ha!
You can't be almost unique!
Unique means one!
You can't be almost one.

**Yes, you can.
Compared with millions, two is <u>almost</u> one.**

Wrong!
Two is <u>twice</u> one.
Therefore not unique.

I said <u>almost</u> unique.

So there are only two of you?

I didn't say so.

So how many of you are there?

I think I'll have a lie down now.

I fancy a tangerine.
Just a segment will do.

Anything else, my lord?

No ... not for the moment.
Coffee later ... perhaps.
You could bring up the paper.
The Racing Section will do.
Oh, and you'd better get me some
Peach Blossom Bath Foam.

Look!
I'm not made of money, you know.
I've spent nearly a week's pocket money on
your precious sliced white, your PG Tips,
your Gold Top and your beloved marmalade.

You pinched the beer.

I didn't pinch it!
It was left over.
It's been there for ages.
It was covered in dust.

The dust is irrelevant.
The beer was not yours.

Ha!
You received stolen goods, then!
That's a crime.
You could go to prison for that.

I did not know the beer was stolen.
I thought it was a gift to a welcome guest.

Welcome! Huh!
Don't kid yourself, Man.
I didn't <u>welcome</u> you in.
I <u>took</u> you in.
Out of pity!

No, you didn't.
I walked in.

You can't just walk into other people's houses!

I can.

Breaking and Entering!
It's a crime!

I didn't break in.
The window was open.

Burglary, then!

But I haven't stolen anything ...
Everything I've had has been freely given.

It's early closing Wednesday, don't forget.

Freely demanded, you mean

"Ask and it shall be given unto you."
Any more tangerine?

JOHN!
DON'T SLAM DOORS!

Sorry, Mum.
Going out.

Ah me!
I wonder what's running at Kempton Park?

Here!
You couldn't put a bet on for me, could you?

No.

The two-thirty at Kempton Park?

I don't know how to.

Charley's Aunt is 8 to 1.

It's probably illegal.

Very good odds.

I'm too young to do it.

Trained by Phil Higgins.
Where's the nearest betting shop?

I've no idea.

Wouldn't take you a minute …

I'm too small to go myself.

You haven't got any money!

Oh no … that's right.
Here … you couldn't … um … could you?

You've got a - moneybox …
haven't you?

I thought all kids had moneyboxes …

Yes. My money seems to have been going down rather fast lately.
I can't think why.

So, it's no?

Yes, it's NO!

All right, all right.
No need to shout.
Only asking nicely …
Wouldn't mind another bicky …

I dreamed about chips last night
Haven't had chips for ages.

Oh, yes?

Don't you like chips?

Yes, quite.

Good!
We could have chips then!
Nearly lunch time.
Mum's gone.

Chips would stink the place out.
Besides, I told you I'm not allowed to fry.

Isn't there a Take Away?
A Chinese? A chippy?

Stop stroking my ankle!

I could come with you, Master.
In your pocket.

Stop kissing my hand!
I've hardly any money left -

Let's blow it all on a chippy blowout!
Lashings of vinegar, salt and tomato ketchup!
Go on. It wouldn't cost you much.
I can only eat about four chips.
Go on.
Please, Master … oh Holy One.
You are so wise, so handsome -

Shut up, you little twerp!

I'll be as good as gold afterwards.
No messes.
No phoning -
Oh … by the way …
Somebody may be calling me -

What!

You'd better take it.

So you did get through!

Oh, no.

You must have done.

Oh, no.
It was engaged.
I told you.

How do they know our number, then?

Directory Enquiries, of course.

Ha!
But how do they know our name
and address?

I told them.

You just said you didn't get through!

I didn't.
I told them before I came.

What!
You knew you were coming here?

Of course.
We don't just wander about, you know.

Look, when you first came here …

Yes?

How did you know I would be …
well … sympathetic?

Oh, I've had my eye on this place for ages.

Really?

**Oh, yes.
Been in and out loads of times.**

What!

**Yes, couple of months or more.
Sussed the place out - nice and warm, clean.
Mum out a lot. Dad out from seven till eight.
No dog. No cat. No baby children.
No vermin.
<u>Very</u> nice boy.
Kind, quiet, generous, sensitive, sweet-natured -**

Shut up!

**Oh yes, I marked this one down
as a good billet weeks ago.
Spent Christmas here.**

You what!

**Yes! Not half!
Loads of good grub.
No health muck then!
That Christmas pud your Mum made!**

Yes!
Mum said she thought mice
had got at the turkey.

That was me.

But I never saw you.

**'Course not. Didn't want you to.
So when this emergency occurred
I came straight over here.**

What emergency?

**Oh, nothing.
Personal matter …
Had to depart …
Sharpish.**

Leaving your clothes?

More or less.

Ssh! Listen!
Mum's key in the door!
Quick! Into the cupboard!

**Don't rush me.
I'm an old man.**

Ssh!
Bedroom door's open.

JOHN!
ARE YOU THERE?

Not supposed to rush about at my age.

Shut up!

JOHN!
ARE YOU IN?

Yes, Mum.
Hullo.

MRS MARTIN SAID SHE SAW
YOU DOWN THE SHOPS.

Oh?
Oh, yes.

YOU WEREN'T BUYING SWEETS,
WERE YOU?

No …
Oh, no …

WHAT <u>WERE</u> YOU BUYING?

Er …
Just a … a comic.

SHE SAID YOU HAD A BAG
OF CHIPS.

Oh really?
Did she?
Oh, yes … I met Darren.
He gave them to me …
he was full up.

A LIKELY STORY.

Despite all your luxurious possessions,
I don't envy you.
You have to live in your parents' pocket.

You live in <u>my</u> pocket.
You're entirely in my power.

Oh no, I'm not.
I can walk out of here any time I like,
<u>You</u> can't.
You're trapped.
<u>I've</u> got my freedom.

Go on, then!
Go!
Go now!

I don't choose to.
I quite like it here.

I bet you do.
Waited on hand and foot.

I'm growing quite fond of you, boy.

Huh!

I enjoy our little arguments.
I always win.

You do not!

I'm older and wiser, of course.

Your brain is the size of a pea!
Your whole head is only the size
of a ping-pong ball.

Oh, dear!
Now you're being childish again.
I will read. Pass the Racing page.

Here you are!

You've got no manners!

Wouldn't you like another bath?

No.
Only just had one.

Two days ago.

That's what I mean.

Sure?

Yes.

No one can say I didn't try.

What?

Nothing.

I'm dying for a bit of roast beef.
Can't you get me some?

We don't have much meat.
Mum's a vegetarian.
Dad's going that way.
She's working on him.

Vegetarians! Pah!
We could roast it up here.
In the fireplace.
Mum won't be back till six.

OK.
I'll try if you like.
It's the very last of my money.

Good oh!
You're a wonder boy!

JOHN!
FOR HEAVEN'S SAKE!
JUST COME DOWN HERE AND LOOK
AT THIS MESS EVERYWHERE.
AND IT'S MARMALADE AGAIN!
HAVE YOU GONE MARMALADE MAD?
YOU REALLY ARE IMPOSSIBLE, JOHN!

I'm fed up!
Always getting told off because of you!
It's not fair!
I get all the blame.
You've got the perfect alibi -
no one knows you exist!
All because I did a good deed and took you in.

**You didn't take me in.
I came in.**

I let you stay, then.

**Yes, but why?
That is the question.**

I felt sorry for you, of course.
You were cold … starving …

You were being kind?

Er … yes.
I suppose I was.

You'd have done the same for anyone?

Yes, I suppose so.

My size didn't come into it?

No.

You weren't attracted … fascinated … by my size?

Well … not just that -

**Suppose you'd been woken up by a naked
starving man six foot tall?
You'd have screamed, run for Mum and Dad
and called the police?**

Yes.

You wouldn't have hid him and fed him?

No.

**So it was just my size?
Not me.
To you I'm small, sweet, fascinating, and lovable.**

Ha!
Lovable! You!

**A toy … a little pet … a human hamster?
Why don't you buy a little plastic wheel
for me to run round on?**

Shut up!

**That's all I am to you.
I'm not a person at all.
I'm a PET!**

ZZZZZZZ...

Evening, boy.

Evening, Man.
Look ... sorry about this afternoon.

Yes, me too.
I forgive you.

What!

Yes. I do. I honestly do.
I've thought long and hard about it.
Prayed for ages.
Didn't sleep a wink in my kip.
I forgive you, my boy.

You are unbelievable.

I know.
I was amazed myself.
The power of prayer, eh?
Now, what's for tea tonight?
Any chance of a <u>fried</u> egg?

I'll go down and see.

FOR HEAVEN'S SAKE!
HAS ANYONE SEEN MY ANTIQUE
SHERRY GLASS? THE ONE WITH
THE HANDLE?

Oh yes ... Dad ...
I took it upstairs.

DAMMIT!
WHATEVER FOR?

Er ... I just wanted to ... look at it.
It's so ... old, and ... beautiful.
I want to draw it.

OH, REALLY?
I SEE ...

Brilliant you getting it, Dad!

YES, YES ... OK.
BRING IT DOWN, WILL YOU
PLEASE, JOHN?

Thanks to you, I've got to have my dinner
in my room.

Oh goody!

There's no goody about it.
It's a punishment.

What for?

Oh nothing much - just getting marmalade
everywhere - on the phone,
on the telly control -

Never mind.
What you got?

Chicken and chips and peas.

Chips!
Yummy!

You're not getting any.
We're only allowed chips once a week.

Oh, come on!
Three chips are a bellyful for me.

All right, then.
Go on.

Just a bit of chick-chick?

No!
It's my dinner.

Tiny bit of skin, Master?
Oh Glorious One.

OK, go on, idiot.
Hey!
Not _that_ much!
Get your feet off my plate!
You're paddling in my gravy!
Are your feet clean?

Nice peas.
Any seconds?

No.
That's part of <u>my</u> punishment
for <u>your</u> crimes.

Any pud?

Apple tart.

Yummy!
Ice cream with it?

No.

Custard, then?

No.

What with it?
There must be <u>something</u> with it?

Goats' Live Natural Yogurt.

Oh, blimey.

Belgian. Un-sweetened.

Oh, no ...

Can we play for money?

No! You haven't got any.

HEY!
WHAT'S THIS?
MY STYLUS BRUSH IS
COVERED IN WHITE STUFF!
FOR HEAVEN'S SAKE -
IT LOOKS LIKE TOOTHPASTE!
WHAT ON EARTH IS GOING ON
IN THIS HOUSE?

Can I come in for a cuddle?

No, you can't!

Go on.

No!
Get off the bed!

I get very lonely.
Can't you just hold me?

No.

Can I just sit in your hand?
Please?

Oh … all right.
Go on, then.

Can we have the nightlight on?

Thanks.
Put your other hand round.
That's better.
Nice and warm.
Feel safe here.
It's a dangerous place - the world … for us …
people like me.
Cats, dogs, birds, foxes, young children, rats,
drain holes, lavatories, feet …
You see, we can't lead a normal life.
Can't go to work,
can't get on a train or bus, can't go about
in crowds. Can't even post a letter …
I haven't seen anyone for ages …
except for one person …
there's not many of us left …
I keep trying to make contact.

Is that what the phoning is about?

Yes.
That and my clothes.

Better turn in now.
Goodnight, boy.

Goodnight, Man.

At last!
I've got it!
You're a refugee, aren't you?

A refugee?

Yes!
You're escaping from oppression,
tyranny and whatnot -

**I hope you're not suggesting I'm a foreigner?
Can't stand foreigners!**

Hah!
You can't stand foreigners!
And you expect me to welcome you
with open arms.

I'm not a foreigner!

You're foreign to this house.

**Oh, I see.
This is a private kingdom, is it?
The wogs begin at the front door?**

Don't use words like that here.
Mum would kill you.

**She sounds like a nice, tolerant liberal sort.
Typical vegetarian.**

Oh, shut up.

Besides, who says you're not
a foreigner?

I speak English, don't I?

So do lots of foreigners.

I'm white, aren't I?

So are lots of foreigners.
Besides you look very brown to me.
And hairy.
Hmm … could be a tan.
Or you could be Asian.

**I am not brown!
I am not Asian!
I was born here!**

So were lots of Asians.

**Huh!
They weren't born here like I was.**

Put your arm out.

I'm not a foreigner!

Hmm … let's look at you.

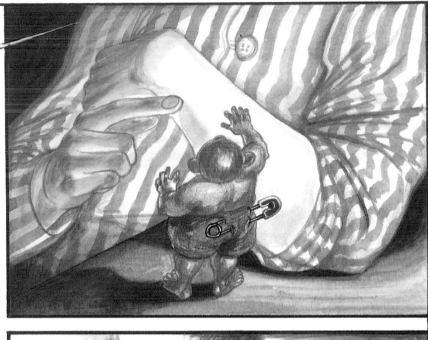

There!
See!
Brown as a nut!

Perhaps you're a different species
altogether …
I'm Homo Sapiens and you are …
Homo … Brownie Boy …
Titchy Twit –

I am not brown!
I am not titchy!
Can't stand foreigners. I like my own sort.
Can't stand <u>your</u> sort either - great big
monsters barging about bashing up
the world.
Who do they think they are?
Human beings!
Can't stand 'em. NONE OF 'EM!

You are unbelievably <u>awful</u>.
Do you know that?
You've just said you can't stand the
whole human race.
I'm going to have to chuck you out.

Go on, then!
Intolerant, that's what you are.
No freedom of speech in this house!
No Human Rights here!
Persecuted for my beliefs!
Now I am to be exiled!
I arrive starving … naked …
I throw myself on your mercy …
Now you shout at me …
Squeeze me up …
Throw me out into the cold snow …

OW!
My eye!

Hard luck.
There's no snow.
It's drizzling -
Oh, never mind …

Get me down.

Get yourself down.

Can't.

Slide down the curtains.

Can't.

Tough.

PETER –

MMM …

I'M SO WORRIED ABOUT JOHNNY …

MMM … WHY?

HE'S BEEN ROASTING MEAT IN HIS ROOM.

WHAT!

YES, HE LIT A FIRE AND ROASTED LUMPS OF
BEEF ON A BIT OF WIRE AND HE BOUGHT A PINT
OF GOLD TOP OFF THE MILKMAN AND HIS OWN
PACKET OF TEA - PG TIPS – AND HE'S TAKEN
TO BUYING HIS OWN EXPENSIVE MARMALADE,
FRANK COOPER'S (SOB) OXFORD (SOB)
MARMALADE (SOB) … WHAT'S HAPPENING
TO HIM - OUR SON? OUR LITTLE BABY? (SOB)

DARLING …
DON'T CRY … SWEETHEART.
IT'S PROBABLY JUST A PHASE.
THOUGH WHY HE CLEANS HIS TEETH WITH
MY STYLUS BRUSH AND PLASTERS THE HOUSE
WITH MARMALADE …

MAYBE I'VE BEEN OVERDOING THE VEGGY
BUSINESS …
HE MIGHT BE A BORN CARNIVORE (SOB)
AND HE'S TAKEN TO DRINK -

WHAT!

I FOUND A HALF-EMPTY BOTTLE OF GUINNESS
UNDER HIS BED.

OH, MY GOD!

You're a Fascist, aren't you?

What?

I bet you're a Nazi. On the run.
You've come here to hide.

I had a rough time in the War.

Oh? Where were you?

I don't talk about it.

Why not?

Too painful.

Sorry.
Which side were you on?

I won a medal.

Really?

Yeah!

Terrific.
What were you in?

Very hush-hush.

Well, what?

**Secret Service Intelligence
Commandos.**

You're a hopeless liar.

Goodnight,
Man.

**Goodnight,
boy.**

THURSDAY

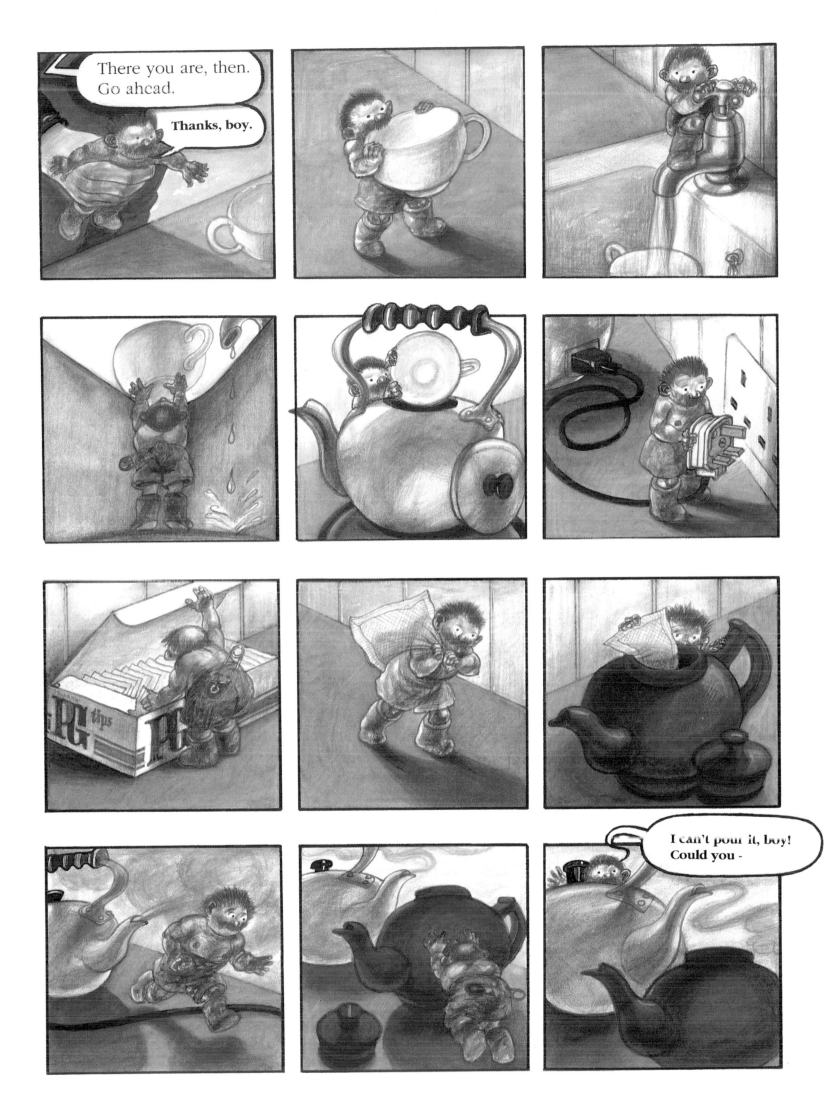

Mum's chucked out your
precious sliced white.
Here's the marge.
And your beloved marmalade.
Just eat it.
Try not to let it get
out of control.
Now I'm going up to read.
Some of us have to work.
I've got a project to do.

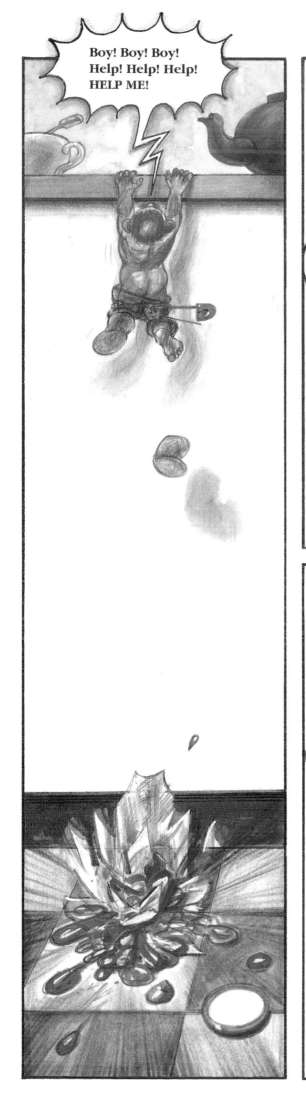

Oh sorry! Sorry, Man.
I shouldn't have left you.

Nearly fell on the glass.

Don't cry.
It's all right. It's all right.

Nearly killed.

No, no, you're all right.
I've got you.
Don't cry.

Nearly died.

You're all right.
Now … there … there …
You have a lie down and
I'll make you a nice breakfast,
OK?

Choccy bicky?

Yes.
Choccy bicky.

Feeling better now?

Yes, not bad.
Been listening to the radio
but it's gone dead.

Oh heck!
You've flattened the batteries!

Oh dear, have I?

My torch is dead, too!

Dear me, is it?
I'm not used to these expensive modern gadgets.
It's easier for you.
You've been brought up on luxuries.
I've always preferred the simple life.

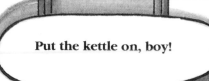

Put the kettle on, boy!

What am I - a waiter?
Waiter … cook … cleaner … shopper …
housewife … baby sitter … nanny …
What _is_ this?
What have I let myself in for?
It's not as if I was a girl …
Girls love cooking …
mothering little things …
dollies … kittens …
they love cleaning up little messes …
I don't want a dolly!

Is that kettle on, boy?

Who does he think he is?

And a choccy bicky!

"Choccy bicky!"
Is that supposed to bring out the
mother in me?

**Make some more tea when that kettle
boils. Good and strong mind!**

This is like having a baby.
I'm too young to be a father!
He's far worse than Grandad.
It's not as if he's that old -

Hurry up with that tea!

There he goes again.
What's more <u>I'm</u> paying for it.
He should be paying <u>me</u>!
When will this end?

**About time.
I thought it was never coming.**

This isn't a hotel, you know.
And try not to make so much mess.

I need a bath.

You're telling me.

What?

Nothing.
I'll get the bowl.

I like watching you eat.

Do you?

Yes.

You like watching me eat.
You like watching me drink.
How would you like to be watched all the time?
I'm not on a stage!
I'm not an actor!
This is me!
This is MY LIFE!
I don't want you turning it into a PERFORMANCE!
Go and watch the telly if you want entertainment.
Don't watch ME!
I REFUSE TO BE ENTERTAINMENT!
I AM ME!

I like that!
I've been like a mother to you.
I've cooked for you!
Bathed you!
Clothed you!
Cleaned up your babyish messes!

Don't try and be noble!
You enjoyed it!
You were fascinated!
You weren't being kind.
You weren't being generous.
You were PLAYING!
Playing with a NEW TOY!
I will not be anyone's TOY!

You exploit your smallness.
You know how to use it.
You manipulate people by it.
You manipulate me for your own selfish ends.
Huh!
You've been having a very cushy time here.
Waited on hand and foot.
Pampered like a baby.
My room is not a HOTEL!
I will not be anyone's SERVANT!
You try to make out you are a dear, sweet,
helpless little chappie when you are really
a bossy, messy, selfish, smelly, calculating
little RAT!

You make out you are being kind, generous
and caring when all you are doing is using
my smallness for your own ENTERTAINMENT.
You don't care for me as a PERSON!
To you, I'm just an entertaining NOVELTY!
You are like all children with their pets.
The novelty soon wears off.
They don't really like animals.
They like NOVELTIES!
I refuse to be a NOVELTY!
And if I am a rat,
then you are a PET RAT KEEPER!
And I know which I would rather be.
A rat has more dignity than its keeper.

Stop shouting!
Dad's home this afternoon.
They're both in!

Who cares?
Goodnight!

Goodnight, rat!

JOHN!

Yes, Mum?

HOW'S THE PLAY GOING?

Play?

IT SOUNDS AS IF YOU'VE GOT HALF
A DOZEN PEOPLE IN YOUR ROOM
SOMETIMES …SHOUTING …
AND CARRYING ON -

Oh, the play!
Yes!
There's a lot of arguing in it.
Mr Timpson says conflict is
the essence of drama.

TALKING OF DRAMA -
YOUR FATHER WANTS
TO TALK TO YOU.
NOW.
AT ONCE.

Oh-oh.
It's bad when she
calls him Father.
OK, Mum.
Coming, Dad!

Phew!
I've just had a terrific ticking off from Dad.

Oh? Why?

Why!
Your beef. Your beer. Your stereo toothbrush.
Your fiddling with the thermostat. Your
marmalade gummed all over everywhere.
And I get the blame!
Now he's stopped my pocket money because
he thinks I'm spending it on drink!
So it's goodbye to all your little luxuries, Man!
And Mum is making a terrific stink about the smell.

Smell?
What smell?
The beef?

No!
Your smell.

My smell?

Yes!
You smell.
Didn't you know that?

Well, everybody smells a bit …

You STINK!

Oh … sorry … I … have baths …
when I can …
think I'll turn in …
have a bit of a kip …

Coast clear?
Mum and Dad?

Gone to a meeting.
I've just been hearing about people
like you on the radio.

Oh?

Yes.
It mentioned you.

Me?

People like you - "in need of care
and protection".
People "at risk".

I'm not at risk!
I'm not in need of care and protection!

It made me realise …
it suddenly dawned on me …
I'm your Social Worker!

They do a lot of hard graft, social workers.

Yes!
Don't I know it.
I'm thinking of handing you over …

What?

Handing you over …
to the Local Authority

No!

They'd put you in a Home.

No!
Not going!
You wouldn't -
What you got the phone in here for?

Lots of nice nursies to look after you.
You'd be their little favourite -
Tiny Tim.

Shut up!
Not going in a Home!

I'll give them a call … tell them I've got a vagrant on the premises
… some old tramp … wandered in off the streets …
stark naked … must be a bit confused … keeps singing hymns …
reads the Bible out loud … bit childish -
keeps asking for marmalade … messy … smelly …
severe physical handicap -
can't even make a cup of tea without killing himself …
they'll get the picture …
obviously in need of care and protection …
definitely at risk …
Ah! Here we are -
Age Concern, Homes for the Elderly,
Community Homes - 07918 …
give them a ring …
just a quick call …
get them to take you away …
0…7…9…1…8 -

NO, BOY!
NOT THE AUTHORITIES!
PLEASE!

I'll be good, honestly.
No more phoning.
No more marmalade.
You won't know I'm here.
I'll hide in the cupboard. Never come out.
Just give me a bit of grub now and again.
I'll be ever so good.
Don't phone the Authorities, please!
I'll pretend I'm a hamster.
Please?
Boy?

OK.
I'll relent.
But remember, I've only got to pick
up the phone.

And I've only got to pick up
a MATCH!

When you and Mummy and Daddy are all
in beddy-bies!

What are you talking about?

I know where the paraffin is.
The turps.
The petrol for the mower.

What!

Wouldn't take a minute.

You said I'd got the perfect alibi, remember?
No one knows I exist!
Then you'd be homeless!
Like me, eh?
You'd be in need of "care and protection".
So just watch it, boy!
YOU ARE "AT RISK"!

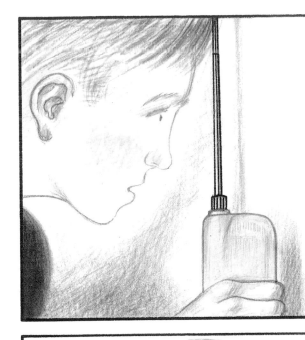

Do you realise what you have just said?

Yes.

You could kill us all.
Mum … and Dad … and me -

<u>You</u> were going to kill <u>me</u>!
Putting me in a Home.
I'd die in a week.

You are ready to kill three people.

<u>You</u> started it.
You threatened to kill <u>me</u>.

You are a murderer.   **You are a murderer.**

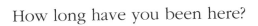

How long have you been here?

Three days.
This is the fourth.

I'm going out for a walk.

So am I.

FRIDAY

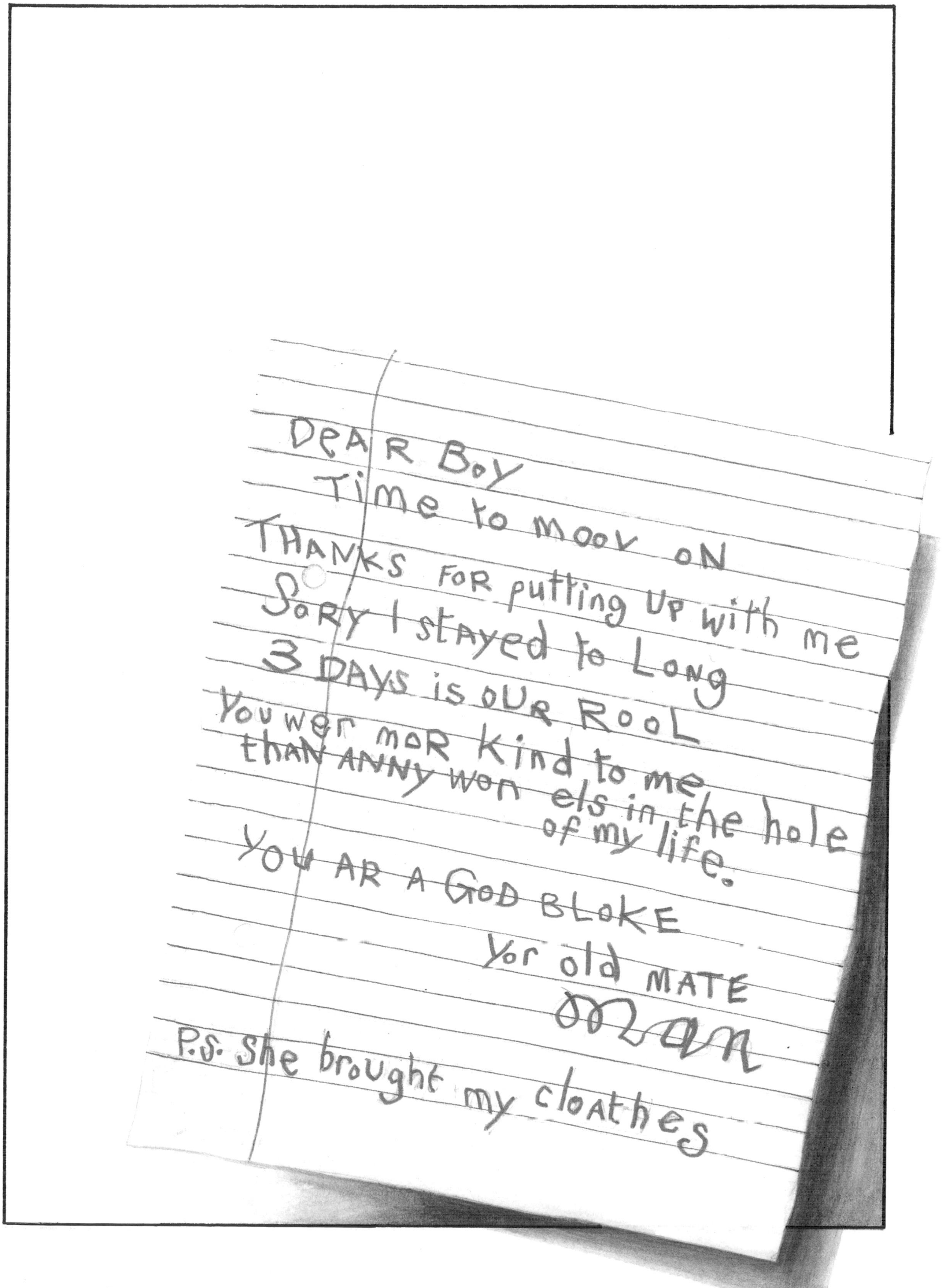

DEAR BOY
Time to moov oN
THANKS FoR putting up with me
SoRY I stayed to Long
3 DAYS is oUR RooL
You wer moR kind to me the hole
thaN ANNY won els in the hole
of my life.

YOU AR A GoD BLoKE
Yor old MATE
man

P.S. she brought my cloathes